Cover layout by Edward Gehlert.
Cover art by Steve Miller.
Interior layout by Edward Gehlert.
Beta Reading by Eva Gehlert.
Editing services provided by Edward Gehlert.

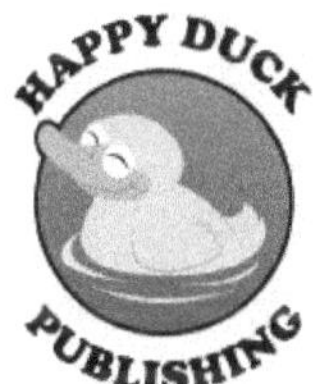

Happy Duck Publishing
111 East 3rd Street
Belle, MO 65013

Genre: Fiction, General
ISBN: 978-1-7369596-2-6
First Edition.

Dream Lover: Looking Back

When I first came to the University of the Arts in Philadelphia in the fall of 1997, everything felt so new. The prior year I had co-written my first screenplay with my friend Steven Rinestine, and now I was attending one of the only programs, at that time, dedicated to screenwriting in the country. There were only a handful of us in the classroom, and our teacher Steve Saylor was tough. I quickly developed a pretty heavy drinking problem, and after my father had a heart attack the following spring, I decided to return home to spend time with family in Pittsburgh and produce my own films, which I did, working with UArts alum John Devennie and meeting my longtime friend and collaborator Chris Lance from Paladin Knight Pictures in the process, while at the same time being named a finalist for the Chesterfield Film Writers Project, which was then sponsored by Steven Sielberg's Amblin Entertainment.

Fast forward to the fall of 1999, and I'm back in the city. I enter the classroom and am greeted by a man in his mid-fifties wearing a fishing vest and a pair of aviator sunglasses in the form of legendary Hollywood screenwriter Charlie Purpura. I did know it then, but Charlie was going to change my life. While he would only have two films produced in his lifetime, ***Heaven Help Us***, starring Andrew McCarthy and Donald Sutherland and ***Satisfaction***, starring Julia Roberts and Justine Bateman, he also had colorful stories about arm wrestling Linda Hamilton during a rewrite on ***Terminator 2***, or shepherding the screenwriters of the film ***While You Were Sleeping***, and getting it from script to screen or working as a credit arbitrator for the W.G.A. More than anything though, he was a mentor.

While I had fought past professors in the program, we just seemed to fit. He was kind and having been raised by a single mother in the 1940's and 50's, had never lost his working class roots. The first semester I knew him we simply explored the idea behind my story, a man who only exists as a character in his girlfriend's dreams, and by the time spring break was over I had a draft that was nearly 100 pages long. It was Charlie who suggested the title, believing that it was always a good thing to be able to tie a famous song to the finished film.

In the age of films like ***Being John Malkovich*** and ***Memento***, Charlie thought that this was a script that might really get some attention and for a while it did. First optioned by Ned Stuart's Lang Syne Films in New York, the script would make its way into the hands of folks like Jackie Chan, Paul Thomas Anderson, Robert Downey Sr., Julia Roberts and DwarfStar Productions founder Brian D. Kline, himself a little person, who fought tooth and nail to see this happen. I did get small offers from a few different independent producers after that, but for whatever reason they never felt right, and so the script went unproduced and when Charlie passed away in 2005, I was left with a profound sense of loss that he would never get to see it become a reality.

In the years that followed I wrote a treatment for the late Rodney Dangerfield and worked for Artlander Productions producer Theron Fairchild on a loose screen adaptation of Frankenstein, which also didn't get made, before finding my way to Paladin Knight Pictures, who adapted my short film ***Buffalo Diamonds*** into a feature length project and recently produced my script ***Missouri Loves Company***, which is awaiting release. I even found another close mentor in the late Blake Snyder, who wrote the film, ***Stop or My Mom Will Shoot!***

While these things are all pretty great, it has always been a source of great heartache that ***Dream Lover*** has never seen the light of day. So now here it is in book form, a love letter to a mentor and a friend that I hope will produce a staged reading or money from possible investors or just readers who are willing to check out the story and hold it close.

All I can say is, if you like what you've read drop me a line, and Charlie, this one's for you.

FADE IN:

EXT. BOARDWALK-NIGHT

A MAN can be seen through a pair of binoculars. He's wearing a cowboy outfit, and twirling a pair of pistols.

TWO DWARFS sit in a golf cart. They are OTIS and RABELAIS.

OTIS is looking through the binoculars. They begin fighting. RABELAIS starts choking OTIS.

RABELAIS
(excited)
Let me see!

The MAN enters a strip club, and a few seconds later some lights go on above it.

OTIS smacks RABELAIS. He falls out of the golf cart.

RABELAIS
(continuing)
Is it him?

RABELAIS brushes himself off. He grabs a hold of the golf cart.

OTIS starts to drive away.

INT. LIONEL'S APARTMENT-MORNING

An alarm clock is blaring. LIONEL rolls out of bed, and falls on the floor. He stumbles to the kitchen.

There is a loud banging noise. LIONEL walks into the next room. The front door bursts open. It smacks him in the face.

His LANDLORD enters.

LANDLORD
Where's my money?!

Blood slowly trickles down LIONEL'S face. Playing cards are scattered everywhere.

LIONEL
(weak smile)
Is that a hypothetical question?

The LANDLORD removes a large pair of fuzzy dice from his coat, and proceeds to box LIONEL'S ears with them. He takes LIONEL'S cowboy hat, and places it on his head.

LANDLORD
(disgusted)
Next time, don't bet more than you can afford to lose.

The LANDLORD exits. His final words echo in LIONEL'S head.

LIONEL walks into the bedroom.

He glances at a framed photo of a YOUNG WOMAN, his girlfriend MARIA.

He removes some money from a purse sitting on the dresser.

Snoring can be heard.

LIONEL exits the room.

EXT. BOARDWALK-MORNING

LIONEL walks along the boardwalk. He begins coughing, and looks at his watch.

INT. THE IRISH PUB-MORNING

LIONEL walks inside. He is still coughing.

His friend TROY DEVENS sits at the bar. He motions LIONEL over.

TROY
Could you spot me a few bucks?

LIONEL continues to stand there coughing. He hands TROY his wallet.

TROY removes a few bills, and places them on the bar. He gets up to leave.

TROY
(continuing)
Thanks.

LIONEL downs what remains of TROY'S drink.

LIONEL
What happened to your wallet?

TROY just smiles, and puts on his coat.

LIONEL yells out after him.

LIONEL
(continuing)
Where are you going?

TROY doesn't turn around.

TROY
Protect and serve Lionel, protect and serve.

LIONEL sits there, and lights a cigarette.

INT. WILD WEST CASINO-MORNING

LIONEL walks into a dark room. A poker game is already in progress.

A MIDDLE AGED MAN in a navy suit walks toward LIONEL.

CASINO MANAGER
(concerned)
What happened to you last night?

LIONEL sighs.

LIONEL
Cold cards.

LIONEL goes over to sit. The CASINO MANAGER places a hand on his shoulder.

CASINO MANAGER
I can't let you sit. You know employee policy.

LIONEL rolls his eyes, and crosses his fingers.

LIONEL
I'll just watch.

LIONEL and The CASINO MANAGER sit watching the card game.

CASINO MANAGER
(to LIONEL)
You look like an unmade bed that got into a bar fight.

LIONEL sits in his wrinkled cowboy outfit. He picks specks of dry blood from his face.

CASINO MANAGER
(continuing)
Where's your hat?

OTIS and RABELAIS sit there playing poker. Each wears a pair of black sunglasses, and a matching trench coat.

The CASINO MANAGER gets up to leave. He hands LIONEL some money, and gives him a knowing glance.

CASINO MANAGER
(continuing)
Just clean yourself up.

LIONEL nods.

The CASINO MANAGER exits.

LIONEL looks around the table, and throws down his money.

LIONEL
Who's deal?

EXT. OUTSIDE THE CASINO-DAY

LIONEL stands brushing a horse.

MARIA walks past him. She is wearing an Indian outfit.

LIONEL runs after her.

LIONEL
(panting)
Wait up!

LIONEL places a gentle kiss on her lips.

MARIA gives him a puzzled look, and then she slaps him.

LIONEL
(continuing)
What the--

MARIA
Who are you?

LIONEL starts laughing.

LIONEL
(smiles)
Funny.

MARIA removes a cigarette from a gold case.

MARIA
(to LIONEL)
Do you have a match?

LIONEL shakes his head. He stands there staring at her.

MARIA
(continuing)
What?!

LIONEL
You don't smoke.

MARIA
Listen, I'm getting tired of your lines. All I wanted was a match.

LIONEL
We have some in the apartment.

MARIA throws her arms up in the air.

MARIA
What are you talking about?!

LIONEL starts pacing around in a panic.

LIONEL
This isn't funny anymore!

INT. WILD WEST CASINO-SAME MOMENT

OTIS and RABELAIS are sitting at slot machines by a window. They watch as LIONEL continues to pace back and forth.

EXT. OUTSIDE THE CASINO-DAY
MARIA places her hands on LIONEL'S shoulders to stop his pacing.

MARIA
It's my first day here! I'm nervous enough!

LIONEL stops in his tracks.

LIONEL
(flustered)
I've got a bottle of scotch.

MARIA softens.

MARIA
(slight smile)
Is that an invitation?

LIONEL starts walking toward his apartment in silence.

MARIA follows him.

MARIA
(continuing)
Do you always go around kissing total strangers?

INT. WILD WEST CASINO-DAY

OTIS and RABELAIS are sitting in a conference room with a THIRD DWARF.

THIRD DWARF
You've seen him?

OTIS and RABELAIS nod. The THIRD DWARF stands holding a pointer. He glances at a pie chart. RABELAIS throws a paper airplane at his head.

THIRD DWARF
(continuing)
Who did that?

The THIRD DWARF stands there pissed. He pops a video into a VCR, and turns on a television.

OTIS sighs.

OTIS
Not again.

The THIRD DWARF pokes him in the eye with his pointer.

THIRD DWARF
(serious)
This is important.

OTIS sits rubbing his eye.

RABELAIS
We're sick of these training videos.

The THIRD DWARF is about to ball out RABELAIS, when a large breasted female dwarf appears on screen. All three of them now sit transfixed.

INT. CLUB WET DREAMS-DAY

LIONEL and MARIA walk through the strip club below LIONEL'S apartment.

LIONEL
Would you like a drink?

MARIA
Shouldn't we be getting back to work?

LIONEL sits down at a table. A waitress comes and sets two napkins down on the table.

LIONEL
I'm sorry about the door.
Wilkinson busted it down this
morning.

MARIA shakes her head, and gets up to leave.

MARIA
(frazzled)
Not this again.

LIONEL points upward.

LIONEL
Our place is upstairs.

MARIA starts walking away. LIONEL decides to play along.

LIONEL
(continuing)
Fine. We've never met. I just
wish we had.

MARIA stops, and sits back down.

LIONEL lights her cigarette.

LIONEL
(continuing)
So where are you from?

MARIA
Iowa, Sioux city.

LIONEL has no idea what to say.

LIONEL
I like corn.

MARIA starts laughing.

MARIA
(smiles)
We didn't live in a cornfield.

MARIA pinches LIONEL. He rubs his arm.

MARIA
(continuing)
I just wanted to make sure I wasn't dreaming.

LIONEL gets up, and slides his chair in.

MARIA
(continuing)
Can I use your bathroom?

LIONEL points upstairs.

INT. LIONEL'S APARTMENT-DAY

LIONEL and MARIA enter the apartment.

LIONEL shows MARIA where the bathroom is.

LIONEL enters his bedroom to get his spare cowboy hat.

MARIA continues to talk to him from the bathroom.

MARIA
So how long have you been working at the casino?

LIONEL is about to place his hat on his head, when he hears snoring. He walks over to the bed, and pulls up the blankets.

LIONEL
(screams)
Maria!

MARIA runs out of the bathroom, and into the bedroom.

LIONEL looks over at her. He faints.

INT. LIONEL'S APARTMENT-LATER

A tea kettle blares.

LIONEL'S eyes open. He sits rubbing his head.

MARIA stands above him.

MARIA
(upset)
What's going on?! Who are you?!

LIONEL sits there mumbling under his breath.

LIONEL
I could ask you the same thing.

MARIA
How do you know my name?!

LIONEL
We met about a year ago on the beach. We've lived here about 3 months.

MARIA paces around the room.

LIONEL grabs a hold of her. He slaps her.

LIONEL
(continuing)
You're making me nervous.

MARIA stands there silently, and attempts to take everything in.

MARIA
(more reasonable)
What's your name?

LIONEL sits down on the floor. MARIA sits down beside him.

LIONEL
You really don't remember?

MARIA nods.

LIONEL
(continuing)
Lionel. Lionel Trimmer.

MARIA points to the spitting image of herself snoring in the bed.

MARIA
Who's that?

LIONEL
That is the question.

INT. CLUB WET DREAMS-DAY

OTIS and RABELAIS are sitting in the club. They are dressed like tourists, wearing very loud Hawaiian shirts.

OTIS
(to RABELAIS)
This was supposed to be my vacation week.

RABELAIS shrugs. A STRIPPER approaches him, and places him between her breasts. She starts shaking him around the room with every jiggle.

INT. LIONEL'S APARTMENT-DAY

LIONEL and MARIA sit talking.

LIONEL
We have to figure out what's going on.

MARIA nods in agreement.

LIONEL mumbles under his breath.

LIONEL
(continuing)
Troy.

MARIA
Huh?

LIONEL notices her puzzled look.

LIONEL
(smiles)
My friend Troy. He's a police detective. Maybe he can figure things out.

MARIA sighs.

MARIA
Let's hope so.

LIONEL and MARIA get up. MARIA looks at the tea kettle.

MARIA
(continuing)
I made you some tea.

LIONEL looks at the tea kettle, and then at MARIA.

LIONEL
It's probably cold by now.

EXT. BOARDWALK-DAY

LIONEL and MARIA walk down the boardwalk on their way to the police station.

LIONEL glances across the boardwalk at a parking garage. He runs toward it.

MARIA
Where are you going?!

INT. PARKING GARAGE-DAY

LIONEL runs into the parking garage. He stares at the ATTENDENT.

LIONEL
Are you undercover?

ATTENDENT
Which car is yours sir?

MARIA runs over to LIONEL.

MARIA
(confused)
What are we doing here?

LIONEL glances at MARIA.

LIONEL
It's Troy.

LIONEL points to the ATTENDENT.

LIONEL
(continuing)
He's Troy.

MARIA looks at his shirt.

MARIA
His tag says Rupert.

The ATTENDENT looks at LIONEL.

ATTENDENT
(baffled)
Do you have a car sir?

LIONEL winks at the ATTENDENT.

LIONEL
If you're on a case, we'll come back later.

ATTENDENT
On a case?

LIONEL
(getting pissed)
Look Troy, it's been a long day. Stop fooling around.

The ATTENDENT looks at MARIA.

ATTENDENT
Talk some sense into your boyfriend here.

LIONEL grabs the ATTENDENT by his shirt.

LIONEL
(screaming)
We need your help Troy! Maria is standing here, and she's sleeping in my bed! They say everyone has a double, but this is really too much!

The ATTENDENT points to his shirt rather violently.

ATTENDENT
The name is Rupert! Rupert Kensington!

LIONEL throws the ATTENDENT to the ground.

He runs out of the parking garage.

The ATTENDENT sits there crying.

EXT. BOARDWALK-DAY

MARIA is running after LIONEL.

MARIA
Now what do we do?

LIONEL stands there silent.

The sound of slot machines can be heard close by.

LIONEL
I need to think.

INT. WILD WEST CASINO-DAY

LIONEL is playing a slot machine.

MARIA is standing beside him.

MARIA
What are we doing here?

LIONEL doesn't even look up at her.

LIONEL
We work here.

MARIA nudges him.

MARIA
I mean, how is this going to help us find out what's going on?

LIONEL continues to stare at the twirling pieces of fruit

across the face of the machine.

LIONEL
This helps me think.

MARIA shakes her head.

MARIA
I have to go to the bathroom.

LIONEL stands there not even noticing that MARIA has left.

OTIS and RABELAIS wander through the casino.

OTIS
We have to get him alone.

RABELAIS nods.

RABELAIS
(frowns)
Those are the rules.

INT. CASINO BATHROOM-DAY

MARIA enters the ladies room.

She looks at her face in a mirror.

She dabs water under her eyes.

OTIS enters the bathroom.

MARIA looks down toward the door, but sees nobody at her eye level.

OTIS
(yells)
Down here sweetie!

MARIA places a hand over her mouth in shock.

OTIS takes a piece of rope from his coat.

MARIA faints.

OTIS
(continuing)
Christ, that was a little too easy.

INT. WILD WEST CASINO-DAY

LIONEL is still playing the slot machine.

RABELAIS pokes his leg.

LIONEL doesn't look away.

LIONEL
This is my machine! Wait your turn grandma!

RABELAIS tries tickling him.

LIONEL swings his leg, kicking him backward across the room.

Moments later, RABELAIS again approaches LIONEL.

This time he bites as hard as he can into LIONEL'S leg.

LIONEL
(continuing)
What the--

LIONEL looks down.

RABELAIS
We need to talk.

LIONEL stares.

RABELAIS
(continuing)
What are you looking at?

LIONEL shakes his head.

LIONEL
Is the circus in town?

RABELAIS gives LIONEL a dirty look.

LIONEL begins to walk away.

RABELAIS
(yells)
I'm talking to you!

LIONEL runs off in search of MARIA.

RABELAIS follows behind him. He runs into the CASINO MANAGER.

CASINO MANAGER
(angered)
Lionel, where have you been all day?

LIONEL
Fred. Listen, I'll explain everything later. Right now, I'm being chased by a midget!

RABELAIS is running toward LIONEL.

RABELAIS
(pissed)
It's dwarf asshole!

RABELAIS tackles LIONEL to the floor.

He starts punching him.

The CASINO MANAGER pulls them apart. He looks at RABELAIS.

CASINO MANAGER
(flustered)
What is this all about?!

RABELAIS stands there pointing a finger at LIONEL.

RABELAIS
(pissed)
He's going to be the end of us all!

The CASINO MANAGER looks at RABELAIS, and motions to LIONEL.

CASINO MANAGER
(to LIONEL)
Just go. I'll take care of our friend here.

LIONEL runs off in search of MARIA.

INT. CASINO BATHROOM-DAY

LIONEL walks in the bathroom in search of MARIA.

EXT. BOARDWALK-DAY

LIONEL runs down the boardwalk.

He then heads panting in the direction of the IRISH PUB.

INT. THE IRISH PUB-DAY

LIONEL walks up to the bar, and orders a beer.

He hands the BARTENDER a few bills.

The BARTENDER quickly throws them back in his face.

BARTENDER
(angered)
What's this?!

LIONEL looks at the bills sitting on the bar, and then up at the BARTENDER.

LIONEL
(puzzled)
I don't understand. What? My money's no good here? I was here this morning!

The BARTENDER reaches into his shirt, and produces a strange form of currency. He sets it on the bar, and points to it.

BARTENDER
(serious)
See this--that's what money looks like.

LIONEL throws his hands up, and grabs the BARTENDER by his collar.

LIONEL
What day is it?

The BARTENDER looks at LIONEL slightly frightened.

BARTENDER
Be serious. You know I can't tell you that.

LIONEL looks at the BARTENDER a second, and then slaps him.

LIONEL
Why not?

The BARTENDER is silent, and then starts crying.

BARTENDER
(sobbing)
Why are you asking me anyway! You already know the answer to your own question!

The BARTENDER continues to stand there sobbing.

LIONEL slaps him again.

LIONEL
(calming tone)
Do you know Troy Devens?

A weak smile comes across the BARTENDER'S face.

BARTENDER
Of course.

LIONEL becomes excited, and slaps his hands down on the bar.

LIONEL
(ecstatic)
Really?!

BARTENDER
Who doesn't?

LIONEL hugs the BARTENDER.

LIONEL
Can you tell where I can find him?

The BARTENDER sighs.

BARTENDER
(pauses)
Sure--I guess.

LIONEL looks at him puzzled.

LIONEL
Is that a problem?

LIONEL raises his hand as if to slap the BARTENDER again.

The BARTENDER looks to ANOTHER MAN at the other end of bar.

BARTENDER
Randy. I'm taking my break now.

LIONEL and the BARTENDER exit the bar.

EXT. BOARDWALK-DAY

LIONEL and the BARTENDER walk down the boardwalk.

The BARTENDER stops in front of an abandoned newsstand.

LIONEL
(confused)
Why are we stopping here?

The BARTENDER lets out a small laugh.

BARTENDER
You said you wanted to find Troy Devens.

LIONEL nods.

BARTENDER
(continuing)
Well, here would be the best place to look.

The BARTENDER starts flipping through large piles of magazines.

LIONEL
(annoyed)
What are you looking for? I need

to find Troy Devens. I've got a problem, and he's the only one who can help me.

The BARTENDER looks up from what he's doing.

BARTENDER
I only wish he could.

The BARTENDER just shakes his head.

BARTENDER
(continuing)
You sure are a strange guy.

LIONEL begins to walk off in the opposite direction.

The BARTENDER waves a magazine up in the air.

BARTENDER
(continuing)
Here it is!

LIONEL stops.

He walks back over to where the BARTENDER is standing.

LIONEL
What have you got there?!

LIONEL grabs a yellowed magazine out the BARTENDER'S hand.

BARTENDER
(smiles proudly)
I told you that I'd help you find Troy Devens.

A frown comes across LIONEL'S face.

He throws the magazine in the BARTENDER'S face.

LIONEL
(pissed)
Is this some sort of joke?

Now the BARTENDER gets angry.

BARTENDER
Troy Devens is no joke! He's the greatest character in detective fiction since Sherlock Holmes!

LIONEL begins to walk away again.

The BARTENDER yells after him.

BARTENDER
(continuing)
Lionel Trimmer is one of our greatest writers!

LIONEL turns around again.

LIONEL
What did you just say?

The BARTENDER just stands there silent.

LIONEL runs over to the BARTENDER, and again grabs him by his collar.

LIONEL
(continuing)
I'm Lionel Trimmer!

The BARTENDER looks at him in disbelief.

BARTENDER
Congratulations.

LIONEL can see the disbelief in the BARTENDER'S eyes.

LIONEL
Really! I am!

LIONEL removes his wallet from his pocket, and hands the BARTENDER his identification.

BARTENDER
(excited)
Wow! I've read all you're stories!

LIONEL walks away.

BARTENDER
(continuing)
I can't wait to tell my friends!

LIONEL doesn't turn around.

INT. LIONEL'S APARTMENT-DAY

LIONEL walks into his apartment.

He goes into the bedroom.

We see MARIA in bed sleeping. He attempts to wake her, but his efforts are futile.

The phone rings in the next room.

LIONEL picks up the receiver of his rotary phone.

LIONEL
(tired)
Hello?

V.O.
Mister Lionel Trimmer?

LIONEL
Yes?

V.O.
(cheerful)
I'm calling to see if you'd be interested in receiving your local newspaper.

LIONEL hangs up the receiver.

LIONEL sits down on his couch.

A few seconds later the phone rings again.

LIONEL
(mad)
I'm not interested!

INT. A VERY SMALL OFFICE BUILDING-DAY

OTIS and RABELAIS sit around a chess board.

OTIS
(evil smile)
You interested in your girlfriend?

We see MARIA tied to a bed with tape across her mouth.

INT. LIONEL'S APARTMENT-DAY

LIONEL gets an amused expression on his face.

LIONEL
She's in bed. Who is this?

INT. A VERY SMALL OFFICE BUILDING-DAY

A gleam of fear comes into OTIS'S eyes.

OTIS
How would you know that?

RABELAIS taps OTIS on the shoulder.

RABELAIS
(whispering)
He's talking about the other one.

OTIS lets out a sigh of relief.

OTIS
I mean the other one.

INT. LIONEL'S APARTMENT-DAY

LIONEL pauses for a second to think.

LIONEL
(playing dumb)
Huh? What do you mean?

INT. A VERY SMALL OFFICE BUILDING-DAY

OTIS throws his phone on the floor.

RABELAIS quickly picks it up.

RABELAIS
What do you mean? We just want to meet with you alone.

OTIS walks over to the bed, and helps MARIA sit up.

She smacks her head on the ceiling. He does this repeatedly. He grabs the phone from RABELAIS.

OTIS
Do you hear that Trimmer? She's gonna have one hell of a headache by the time I'm done.

LIONEL can be heard laughing on the other line.

INT. LIONEL'S APARTMENT-DAY

LIONEL hangs up the phone.

INT. A VERY SMALL OFFICE BUILDING-DAY

OTIS and RABELAIS are sitting playing their game of chess.

OTIS
(sad expression)
What do we do now?

RABELAIS shakes his head.

RABELAIS
I dunno. I still can't believe he didn't want her.

OTIS removes a picture of a rather ugly FEMALE DWARF from his pocket, and sets it down in the middle of the chess board.

OTIS
(smirk)
I can't say I blame him. I wouldn't want two of my girlfriend either.

RABELAIS laughs.

EXT. BOARDWALK-DAY

LIONEL is walking down the boardwalk.

An OLD WOMAN grabs hold of his hand.

LIONEL
(startled)
Listen, I don't have any change.

The OLD WOMAN reaches behind LIONEL'S ear, and produces a coin.

She stands there laughing, and then runs her hands across LIONEL'S palm.

LIONEL
(continuing)
What is this all about?

The OLD WOMAN leads LIONEL into a small building.

INT. PALM READER'S APARTMENT-DAY

We see the inside of a small cluttered apartment.

Many pictures of LIONEL are scattered around the room.

PALM READER
(frowns)
Things have been a little strange lately, yes?

LIONEL looks around the room, and stands there staring at the pictures.

LIONEL
(puzzled)
Have we met before?

The PALM READER claps her hands together, and then motions for LIONEL to sit down on her couch.

PALM READER
You tell me the past, and I'll show you the future.

LIONEL stands there silently.

PALM READER
(continuing)
This is your fortune cookie.

LIONEL
You want to know--you want to know about the past.

The PALM READER places a hand on LIONEL'S head.

She takes his hand, and closes his eyes.

INT. A SMOKY KITCHEN-NIGHT

A group of MIDDLE AGED MEN are playing cards.

A LITTLE BOY stands watching them.

BUZZ
(screams)
Lionel! Daddy's working here!

The LITTLE BOY scampers off.

He stops at the television, and stares at the image of a WESTERN COWBOY.

INT. POLICE ACADEMY BUILDING-DAY

TWO YOUNG MEN sit in cadets uniforms. One holds a newspaper tightly.

YOUNG LIONEL
(in tears)
Troy--I just can't believe it.
John Wayne--dead.

YOUNG LIONEL sits there twirling his gun.

YOUNG TROY
(sympathetic)
You're the last cowboy my friend.

EXT. A DARK ALLEY-EARLY MORNING

TWO YOUNG POLICE OFFICERS run down an alley.

One of them, YOUNG LIONEL, fires his pistol.

We see the image of a DEAD YOUNG BOY.

YOUNG LIONEL stands there in tears.

YOUNG LIONEL
(upset)
Ah, shit! Shit Troy!

YOUNG TROY places his hands on YOUNG LIONEL'S shoulders.

YOUNG LIONEL
(continuing)
Ah. Man I'm a killer--a baby killer.

Tears stream down LIONEL'S face.

YOUNG TROY
(weak smile)
You're a cowboy.

EXT. BOARDWALK-EARLY MORNING

We see a YOUNG LIONEL get off a bus.

He walks past the WILD WEST CASINO, there is a HELP WANTED sign. He goes inside.

YOUNG LIONEL is handed a cowboy outfit by a YOUNG WOMAN, MARIA.

EXT. BEACH-DAY

A YOUNGER LIONEL and MARIA frolic on the beach. They embrace, and look into each other's eyes.

LIONEL
(mouths the words)
I love you.

INT. PALM READER'S APARTMENT-DAY

We see tears running down the PALM READER'S face.

She let's go of LIONEL'S hand, and his eyes open.

PALM READER
(stares at LIONEL)
Now--to the future.

The PALM READER snaps her fingers, and LIONEL disappears in a cloud of smoke.

EXT. BOARDWALK-NIGHT

A MAN can be seen through a pair of binoculars. He's wearing a cowboy outfit, and twirling a pair of pistols.

TWO DWARFS sit in a golf cart. They are OTIS and RABELAIS.

RABELAIS starts choking OTIS.

RABELAIS
(excited)
Let me see!

THE MAN enters a strip club, and a few seconds later some lights go on above it.

OTIS smacks RABELAIS. He falls out of the golf cart.

RABELAIS
(continuing)
Is it him?

RABELAIS brushes himself off. He grabs a hold of the golf cart.

OTIS starts to drive away.

INT. LIONEL'S APARTMENT-MORNING

An alarm clock is blaring.

LIONEL rolls out of bed, and falls on the floor. He stumbles to the kitchen. There is a loud banging noise.

LIONEL walks into the next room. The front door bursts open. It smacks him in the face.

His LANDLORD enters.

LANDLORD
(pissed)
Where's my money?!

Blood slowly trickles down LIONEL'S face. Playing cards are scattered everywhere.

LIONEL
(weak smile)
Haven't we been through this already?

The LANDLORD gives LIONEL a strange look, and then removes a large pair of fuzzy dice from his coat.

He proceeds to box LIONEL'S ears with them. Then he takes LIONEL'S cowboy hat, and places it on his head.

LANDLORD
(disgusted)
Next time, don't bet more than you can afford to lose.

The LANDLORD exits. His final words echo in LIONEL'S head.

LIONEL walks into the bedroom. He glances at a framed photo of a YOUNG WOMAN, his girlfriend MARIA.

He kisses her on the cheek, and then removes some money from a purse sitting on the dresser.

Snoring can be heard.

LIONEL exits the room.

EXT. BOARDWALK-MORNING

LIONEL walks along the boardwalk. He begins coughing, and looks at his watch.

INT. THE IRISH PUB-MORNING

LIONEL walks inside. He is still coughing. His friend TROY DEVENS sits at the bar. He motions LIONEL over.

LIONEL sets some money in front of TROY.

TROY
(amused smile)
What's that for?

LIONEL
You were going to ask me to spot you, right?

TROY gives LIONEL a strange look.

LIONEL
(continuing)
Aren't you on duty?

TROY frowns, and gets up to leave.

TROY
(smiles)
This isn't the old west--there are no more codes of honor.

TROY slaps LIONEL'S shoulder, and puts on his coat. He starts to walk away. LIONEL yells after him.

LIONEL
Aren't you forgetting something?!

LIONEL holds up a weathered badge. TROY smiles, and takes the badge.

TROY
I'll see you later partner.

TROY exits the PUB.

INT. WILD WEST CASINO-MORNING

LIONEL walks into a dark room.

A poker game is already in progress.

A MIDDLE AGED MAN a navy suit walks toward LIONEL.

CASINO MANAGER
(concerned)
What happened to you last night?

LIONEL gives him a puzzled look for a second.

LIONEL
(whispering)
You mean with the dwarfs?
Yesterday sure was odd.

The CASINO MANAGER raises an eyebrow.

CASINO MANAGER
(whispering)
What dwarfs? Why are we whispering?

LIONEL places a hand on the CASINO MANAGER'S shoulder.

LIONEL
(yells)
They took the second Maria!

The CASINO MANAGER looks around the room.

CASINO MANAGER
(slightly frightened)
What do you mean second Maria?

LIONEL'S eyes bulge.

LIONEL
(upset)
They took her!

The CASINO MANAGER puts his arm around LIONEL. He points to a slot machine.

CASINO MANAGER
(smiles)
Maria's right over there.

LIONEL gives off a sigh of relief. He starts to walk toward MARIA. The CASINO MANAGER stops him.

CASINO MANAGER
(continuing)
Aren't you going to play?

LIONEL shakes his head.

CASINO MANAGER
(continuing)
Where's your hat?

MARIA begins to walk off. LIONEL runs after her.

EXT. WILD WEST CASINO-MORNING

MARIA is standing outside the casino in an Indian outfit.

She is looking through her pockets.

LIONEL comes running outside, he falls, and lands on top of MARIA, knocking her over.

MARIA
(rubs her head)
What the--

She looks at LIONEL.

LIONEL
(concerned)
We have to talk.

MARIA sighs.

MARIA
Not you again.

LIONEL becomes excited.

LIONEL
You remember me?

MARIA gets up off the ground, and dusts herself off.

MARIA
How could I not? Lionel, right?

LIONEL quickly gets up.

LIONEL
(excited)
Right! Thank God! I thought this was going to be a repeat of

yesterday.

MARIA slaps LIONEL.

LIONEL
(continuing)
What was that for?

MARIA
(smiles)
Not helping me up. A real cowboy would've.

MARIA slaps LIONEL again.

LIONEL
And what was that for?

MARIA
That was for getting me kidnapped by midgets.

LIONEL gives MARIA a blank stare.

LIONEL
(serious)
They're dwarfs.

MARIA shakes her head.

MARIA
Whatever. What's up with this "other me" business?

LIONEL just stands there scratching his chin.

LIONEL
Did you ask them?

MARIA is staring off blankly.

MARIA
What? No. They had me watch them play Twister.

LIONEL starts laughing.

MARIA
(continuing)
Have you ever seen anything like that? It isn't funny. They said that they had to talk to you alone.

LIONEL
Let's go to my apartment. Maybe there will be some clues there.

LIONEL and MARIA start to walk back toward the apartment.

OTIS and RABELAIS follow behind them.

LIONEL
(continuing)
They're following us.

MARIA stops, and looks at LIONEL.

MARIA
How do you know?

LIONEL starts walking again, and then he stops again.

OTIS and RABELAIS stop very quickly, and trip over each other.

LIONEL
They don't exactly possess the tracking skills of Sam Spade.

MARIA quickly turns around. OTIS and RABELAIS scatter.

MARIA
(laughing)
I see what you mean.

INT. LIONEL'S APARTMENT-MORNING

LIONEL and MARIA enter the apartment. They begin throwing things around looking for clues.

They enter the bedroom, and find the other MARIA there sleeping.

INT. CLUB WET DREAMS-MORNING

OTIS and RABELAIS walk into the club. They sit down at a

table.

Two beers are placed in front of them, and they look up to see the LARGE BREASTED FEMALE DWARF from the training video.

FEMALE DWARF
(smiles)
On the house.

She pinches OTIS on the cheek.

FEMALE DWARF
(continuing)
So cute.

OTIS blushes.

RABELAIS drools.

RABELAIS
(jealous)
Would you stop thinking about tail?! We're on duty!

OTIS lowers his head in shame.

RABELAIS waves a dollar at the FEMALE dwarf, while OTIS'S head is turned. She sticks her tongue out at him, and walks away.

INT. LIONEL'S APARTMENT-MORNING

LIONEL and MARIA have been attempting to wake the other MARIA.

They exit the apartment, and head downstairs.

INT. CLUB WET DREAMS-DAY

OTIS and RABELAIS are now very drunk. They notice LIONEL coming downstairs.

OTIS
(burps)
It's him!

They see MARIA with him, and quickly try to hide.

They run up on the stage.

The FEMALE DWARF picks up a microphone.

FEMALE DWARF
It looks like it's ladies night!

RABELAIS starts to stammer.

OTIS takes off his trench coat, and begins twirling it around.

LIONEL and MARIA watch in amusement.

A large group of woman walk in.

OTIS continues to strip off his clothes, and dance around.

They begin cheering, and then RABELAIS starts dancing as well.

OTIS jumps off the stage, and starts crowd surfing.

LIONEL and MARIA quickly exit the club.

INT. BOARDWALK-DAY

LIONEL and MARIA are standing up against a railing.

MARIA
(puzzled)
Why didn't we stay, and get some answers?

LIONEL shakes his head.

LIONEL
I'm kinda afraid to be alone with those two.

MARIA
(shrugs)
What now?

LIONEL
We find Troy.

MARIA
The parking attendant?

LIONEL
Not Rupert, Troy. He's a detective.

MARIA starts laughing.

MARIA
We're looking for detective--
that's kind of ironic.

LIONEL and MARIA continue walking down the boardwalk.

LIONEL again sees the PALM READER.

PALM READER
(to LIONEL)
Have you seen the future?

The PALM READER takes a hold of MARIA, and wraps her arms around her.

MARIA
(startled)
What the--

PALM READER
(to MARIA)
Poor child.

She grabs one of MARIA'S hands.

She places a hand on MARIA'S head. LIONEL does the same.

EXT. SUBURBAN LAWN-DAY

A LITTLE GIRL sits at a picnic table. She is blowing out candles on a plain looking birthday cake.

She begins to open a present, and then we see that there are a stack of yellowed detective stories inside. She frowns.

INT. AN OFFICE BUILDING-DAY

We see a YOUNG MARIA filing some papers.

EXT. BOARDWALK-EARLY MORNING

We see a YOUNG MARIA get off a bus, and then enter the WILD

WEST CASINO.

EXT. BEACH-DAY

A YOUNGER LIONEL and MARIA frolic on the beach. They embrace, and look into each other's eyes.

MARIA
(mouths the words)
I love you.

EXT. WILD WEST CASINO-NIGHT

LIONEL and MARIA stand talking to the CASINO MANAGER.

CASINO MANAGER
(beaming)
How would you guys like to work the street fair tonight?

LIONEL and MARIA stand there in silence.

CASINO MANAGER
(continuing)
Great!

EXT. STREET FAIR-NIGHT

LIONEL is sitting on a horse.

MARIA walks past him, and places an apple on her head.

LIONEL twirls his pistols.

The crowd cheers.

LIONEL'S horse makes a jerking movement just as he is about to fire.

The gun goes off, and the bullet hits MARIA in the forehead.

She slumps to the ground.

LIONEL runs over to her.

INT. PALM READER'S APARTMENT-DAY

The PALM READER let's go of MARIA'S hand, and MARIA opens her eyes.

The PALM READER looks to LIONEL. She snaps her fingers, and MARIA disappears in a cloud of smoke.

PALM READER
(to LIONEL)
Seek her tomorrow.

The PALM READER again snaps her fingers, and this time LIONEL disappears in a cloud of smoke.

EXT. BOARDWALK-NIGHT

A MAN can be seen through a pair of binoculars. He's wearing a cowboy outfit, and twirling a pair of pistols.

TWO DWARFS sit in a golf cart. They are OTIS and RABELAIS.

OTIS is looking through the binoculars. They begin fighting.

RABELAIS starts choking OTIS.

RABELAIS
(excited)
Let me see!

The MAN enters a strip club, and a few seconds later some lights go on above it.

OTIS smacks RABELAIS. He falls out of the golf cart.

RABELAIS
(continuing)
Is it him?

RABELAIS brushes himself off. He grabs a hold of the golf cart.

OTIS starts to drive away.

INT. LIONEL'S APARTMENT-MORNING

An alarm clock is blaring. LIONEL rolls out of bed, and falls on the floor. He stumbles to the kitchen.

There is a loud banging noise.

LIONEL walks into the next room. The front door bursts open. It smacks him in the face.

His LANDLORD enters.

LANDLORD
(pissed)
Where's my money!?

Blood slowly trickles down LIONEL'S face. Playing cards are scattered everywhere.

LIONEL
(weak smile)
Third times a charm, right?

The LANDLORD removes a large pair of fuzzy dice from his coat, and proceeds to box LIONEL'S ears with them.

He takes LIONEL'S cowboy hat, and places it on his head.

LANDLORD
(disgusted)
Next time, don't bet more than you can afford to lose.

The LANDLORD exits. His final words echo in LIONEL'S head.

LIONEL walks into the bedroom.

He glances at a framed photo of a YOUNG WOMAN, his girlfriend MARIA.

He removes some money from a purse sitting on the dresser.

Snoring can be heard.

LIONEL exits the room.

EXT. BOARDWALK-MORNING

LIONEL walks along the boardwalk.

He begins coughing, and looks at his watch.

INT. THE IRISH PUB-MORNING

LIONEL walks inside. He is still coughing.

His friend TROY DEVENS sits at the bar. He motions LIONEL over.

LIONEL hands TROY his wallet.

LIONEL
(smiles)
Just take what you need.

TROY opens the wallet, and sets a few bills down on the bar.

LIONEL
(continuing)
Listen, we need to talk.

TROY sips his beer.

TROY
So talk partner, I'm listening.

LIONEL stares intensely at TROY.

LIONEL
(serious)
Are you really you?

LIONEL pinches TROY, and himself. TROY winces in pain.

TROY
(startled)
What the—

LIONEL
I think I'm dreaming. Things have been too weird lately.

TROY
(confused)
What are you talking about?

LIONEL
(frantic)
People I know don't seem to know me! I'm being trailed by dwarfs in

trench coats!

TROY
(calm tone)
Slow down cowboy--you need a drink.

TROY places his unfinished beer in front of LIONEL.

LIONEL pushes the mug away. It falls off the bar, and shatters on the floor.

The BARTENDER looks at LIONEL.

BARTENDER
(mad)
Hey!

TROY
(to LIONEL)
What's wrong?

The BARTENDER points his finger at LIONEL.

BARTENDER
You're going to pay for that!

TROY grabs the BARTENDER by his collar.

TROY
Listen pal, Lionel Trimmer can break as many mugs as he likes!

The BARTENDER becomes excited.

BARTENDER
Did you say Lionel Trimmer?

LIONEL throws his face down on the bar.

LIONEL
(muffled)
Not this again.

BARTENDER
Lionel Trimmer the writer?

TROY looks at LIONEL. LIONEL just shrugs.

TROY
No. You have the wrong guy. My friend's a cowboy.

BARTENDER
(to LIONEL)
Like John Wayne?

LIONEL frowns.

LIONEL
No. Definitely not like John Wayne.

The BARTENDER just shakes his head.

BARTENDER
(to LIONEL)
So you didn't write the Maria Caswell stories.

LIONEL sits there staring at him.

TROY is about to answer.

LIONEL puts a hand over his mouth.

LIONEL
(defensive)
What do you know about Maria Caswell?

The BARTENDER gives LIONEL a smug look.

BARTENDER
Every creative writing student worth his salt, knows about Maria Caswell.

LIONEL grabs the BARTENDER by the shoulders.

LIONEL
How's that?

The BARTENDER laughs.

BARTENDER
She's only the greatest character

in detective fiction!

TROY looks at LIONEL.

TROY
(puzzled)
What is he talking about?

LIONEL shakes his head.

LIONEL
I tried to tell you how strange things had gotten.

TROY
(flustered)
This is just freaky.

LIONEL turns his attention back to the BARTENDER.

LIONEL
Could you tell me where I could find any of these Maria Caswell stories?

The BARTENDER looks down at the other end of the bar. ANOTHER BARTENDER stands talking on the phone.

BARTENDER
I'm taking my break.

LIONEL, the BARTENDER, and TROY exit the PUB.

EXT. BOARDWALK-DAY

LIONEL, The BARTENDER, and TROY come upon an abandoned newsstand.

They begin searching through many large stacks of yellowed magazines.

The BARTENDER holds one up in the air.

BARTENDER
(excited)
Found one!

LIONEL grabs it out of his hand.

LIONEL
Let me see that!

The magazine gets ripped.

EXT. BOARDWALK-LATER

LIONEL stands trying to piece the magazine together.

LIONEL
I get to the point where Maria begins to have a dream, but I have no idea what happens after that.

LIONEL glares at the BARTENDER.

LIONEL
(continuing)
This is all your fault!

The BARTENDER just stares at him.

LIONEL
(continuing)
If only you hadn't grabbed the magazine!

All of a sudden, the BARTENDER takes a swing at LIONEL.

BARTENDER
(pissed)
I grabbed the magazine?! You really are living in a dream world! You know that?!

TROY waves his arms up in the air.

TROY
(voice of reason)
Enough! This doesn't help us figure anything out!

LIONEL calms down.

LIONEL
You're right. What now?

TROY
You mentioned something about being trailed by midgets?

LIONEL frowns.

LIONEL
They're dwarfs.

TROY
Whatever. Do you know where we can find them?

LIONEL shrugs.

LIONEL
I have to meet with them alone.

TROY
No way.

LIONEL
Those are their conditions.

TROY sits there thinking things over.

TROY
(smiles)
I'll tail you. Do you think they'll notice?

LIONEL laughs.

LIONEL
Not these guys. If they were dogs, they'd chase their own tails.

Now TROY laughs.

INT. LIONEL'S APARTMENT-DAY

LIONEL and TROY are sitting on LIONEL'S couch. TROY is fitting LIONEL for a wire.

LIONEL
(frowns)
Do I really have to wear this?

TROY nods.

TROY
Yeah. I can't get too close.

LIONEL
Shit.

TROY winces.

TROY
What now?

LIONEL
I have to find Maria. They'll probably try to kidnap her, so that they can get me alone.

TROY
(confused)
Will she remember who you are?

LIONEL
By the end of the day, you won't even remember who I am. She will though.

INT. WILD WEST CASINO-DAY

LIONEL and TROY enter the casino.

MARIA is standing there waiting for LIONEL.

MARIA
(to LIONEL)
Where have you been?

MARIA looks at TROY, and then back at LIONEL.

MARIA
(continuing)
Who's this?

TROY raises an eyebrow.

TROY
(to LIONEL)
She really doesn't know me?

LIONEL gives MARIA a weak smile. He points to TROY.

LIONEL
Maria, this is MR.--

MARIA finishes LIONEL'S sentence.

MARIA
Troy Devens.

TROY shakes MARIA'S hand.

TROY
(to MARIA)
Now all we have to do, is get you kidnapped.

MARIA
Excuse me?

MARIA gives both LIONEL and TROY a puzzled look.

LIONEL
(smiles)
I've got an idea.

Just then the CASINO MANAGER walks over.

CASINO MANAGER
(beaming)
How would you guys like to work the street fair tonight?

LIONEL and MARIA stand there in silence.

CASINO MANAGER
(continuing)
Great!

LIONEL
Maybe later Fred.

A troubled expression comes across the CASINO MANAGER'S face.

CASINO MANAGER
(upset)
What?!

LIONEL starts whispering in MARIA'S ear.

He sits down at the closest card table.

We see OTIS and RABELAIS hiding by a slot machine.

MARIA walks over to the table where LIONEL is sitting.

MARIA
(fake rage)
What do you think you're doing?!

LIONEL pretends to look up startled.

LIONEL
(smiles)
Hey dar--

MARIA
Don't darling me! You spend every dime we have, on what? Gambling!

MARIA forces tears, and runs off toward the bathroom.

OTIS and RABELAIS stand there witnessing the exchange.

OTIS then follows MARIA into the bathroom.

LIONEL continues with his card game.

TROY is now sitting in the game, across the table from LIONEL.

RABELAIS stands watching LIONEL in his element.

INT. CASINO BATHROOM-DAY

MARIA stands washing her face in the sink.

OTIS stands directly behind her.

OTIS
Down here hot stuff.

MARIA pretends to look around a second, and then looks down at OTIS'S smiling face.

MARIA places a hand over her mouth in shock. Then she slumps to the floor.

OTIS removes a piece of rope from his coat.

OTIS
(continuing)
Christ, that was a little too easy.

INT. WILD WEST CASINO-DAY

OTIS peeks his head out of bathroom door. He sees RABELAIS, and motions for him.

INT. CASINO BATHROOM-DAY

RABELAIS enters the bathroom.

RABELAIS throws his arms up in the air. He points to MARIA.

RABELAIS
(to OTIS)
How are we going to move this?!

OTIS and RABELAIS stand there uncertain about how to move MARIA.

OTIS snaps his fingers together.

OTIS
(excited)
I've got an idea!

RABELAIS sighs.

RABELAIS
(sarcastic)
This--should be great. Go ahead Sherlock.

INT. HOTEL RESERVATION DESK-DAY

OTIS and RABELAIS stand in front of the WILD WEST CASINO'S reservation desk.

A DESK CLERK stands helping other people that got there after them.

OTIS
(antsy)
Hey!

The DESK CLERK looks down at them.

DESK CLERK
(snotty)
May I help you gentleman?

RABELAIS gives the DESK CLERK a funny look.

RABELAIS
(pissed)
What's this all about? We need a room.

The DESK CLERK points to a sign with a dwarf on it, and an X through it.

OTIS
(to the DESK CLERK)
We just need a room.

DESK CLERK
(smug)
You know the rules! We don't cater to the small here.

OTIS looks as if he is about to walk away, and then he jumps over the desk.

He starts choking the DESK CLERK.

OTIS
(hostile)
Look, just let us borrow a bellboy then.

The DESK CLERK coughs a little, and then starts laughing.

RABELAIS
What's so funny?

The DESK CLERK gets control of himself.

DESK CLERK
The day bellboy's a drunk. He never showed up today.

OTIS smiles.

OTIS
We'll take you then.

The DESK CLERK gives OTIS a look of repulsion.

DESK CLERK
I have to watch the desk.

OTIS pulls out of badge, and shows it to the DESK CLERK.

DESK CLERK
(continuing)
How can I be of service?

OTIS and RABELAIS lead the DESK CLERK to the bathroom.

They go inside.

INT. CASINO BATHROOM-DAY

MARIA is still on the floor.

DESK CLERK
(continuing)
What's this all about?

OTIS and RABELAIS laugh.

RABELAIS
We need someone to carry our things.

The DESK CLERK looks at them.

DESK CLERK
(uncertain)
Yes?

RABELAIS points to MARIA.

RABELAIS
She's our things.

The DESK CLERK gulps. He pokes MARIA with his shoe.

DESK CLERK
I see.

The DESK CLERK takes MARIA'S arms, and OTIS and RABELAIS take her legs.

INT. WILD WEST CASINO-DAY

They carry her through the casino. The CASINO MANAGER sees them.

CASINO MANAGER
(disturbed)
What's going on here?

DESK CLERK
She passed out sir.

The DESK CLERK points to OTIS and RABELAIS.

DESK CLERK
(continuing)
These fine small gentlemen were helping me take her to her room.

The strain from holding MARIA'S body is too much, and they drop her.

The CASINO MANAGER looks strangely at the three of them.

CASINO MANAGER
Carry on.

The DESK CLERK stammers.

DESK CLERK
Th-tha-thank you sir.

The CASINO MANAGER looks at the DESK CLERK.

CASINO MANAGER
Just be careful.

The CASINO MANAGER walks off.

OTIS, RABELAIS, and the DESK CLERK pick MARIA up again.

DESK CLERK
(to OTIS)
Where are we taking her?

OTIS shakes his head.

DESK CLERK
(continuing)
I really can't give you guys a room.

OTIS gives the DESK CLERK an angry stare.

OTIS
Think of something!

The DESK CLERK'S eyes gleam.

DESK CLERK
(smiles)
There is one room.

RABELAIS
(panting)
Anything will do.

The DESK CLERK points upward.

DESK CLERK
Upstairs.

OTIS, RABELAIS, and the DESK CLERK stand in front of a very small door.

The DESK CLERK fumbles through a large key ring.

He opens the door. Dust flies out. They all start coughing.

MARIA starts coughing.

They all look at her.

DESK CLERK
(continuing)
I thought you guys killed the bitch.

OTIS and RABELAIS just look at him surprised.

MARIA opens her eyes, and continues coughing.

They carry MARIA inside. The DESK CLERK ducks his head.

They throw MARIA on the floor.

OTIS
I'm going to call Trimmer.

RABELAIS nods.

RABELAIS
(to the DESK CLERK)
This place is filthy.

THE DESK CLERK nods in agreement.

DESK CLERK
It belonged to the founder of the casino.

There is a framed photo of a REGAL LOOKING DWARF on the wall.

RABELAIS
I thought you didn't cater to the small?

The DESK CLERK points to the picture.

DESK CLERK
His name was Harry Krumpnik--he hated his own kind.

The DESK CLERK hugs RABELAIS, and they stand there crying.

OTIS is dialing LIONEL'S phone number.

OTIS
(yells)
I can't hear!

INT. LIONEL'S APARTMENT-DAY

LIONEL and TROY sit playing cards.

TROY
(bored)
I hope they--

The phone rings.

TROY
(continuing)
Call soon.

LIONEL picks up the phone.

INT. SMALL HOTELROOM-DAY

RABELAIS and the DESK CLERK set MARIA on the toilet.

OTIS
(smiles)
Is this Trimmer?

INT. LIONEL'S APARTMENT-DAY

LIONEL
(hesitant tone)
Yes?

INT. SMALL HOTELROOM-DAY

OTIS stands there nervously.

OTIS
I have your girlfriend.

Laughing can be heard on the other end of the line.

OTIS
(continuing)
What?!

INT. LIONEL'S APARTMENT-DAY

We see a sleeping MARIA. She is still snoring in bed.

LIONEL
She's right here in front of me.

INT. SMALL HOTELROOM-DAY

OTIS sets down the receiver, and starts screaming.

He picks the phone back up.

OTIS
(yells)
The other one!

INT. LIONEL'S APARTMENT-DAY

LIONEL
(laughing)
What do you want?

INT. SMALL HOTEL-DAY

OTIS
(frazzled)
We need to meet.

INT. LIONEL'S APARTMENT-DAY

LIONEL
Sure.

LIONEL hangs up the phone.

TROY looks at LIONEL.

TROY
Where and when?

LIONEL sighs.

LIONEL
In front of the casino. One hour from now.

TROY checks his watch.

TROY
Perfect. What are you going to say?

LIONEL
(smiles)
Nothing. I'm going to listen.

INT. SMALL HOTELROOM-DAY

RABELAIS and the DESK CLERK stare at OTIS nervously.

RABELAIS
He's coming?

OTIS looks at RABELAIS.

OTIS
(to RABELAIS)
He said sure.

DESK CLERK
That was easy.

OTIS and RABELAIS look at him.

DESK CLERK
(continuing)
I gotta go.

OTIS stands in front of him.

OTIS
We need you to watch the girl.

RABELAIS nods.

OTIS points to the bathroom.

OTIS and RABELAIS lock the DESK CLERK in the bathroom with MARIA.

RABELAIS
(to OTIS)
We have to call the boss.

OTIS nods.

OTIS
You do it.

RABELAIS picks up the phone.

INT. A VERY SMALL OFFICE BUILDING-DAY

The THIRD DWARF is making another group of DWARFS watch the training video.

THIRD DWARF
(coughs)
Hello?

INT. SMALL HOTELROOM-DAY

RABELAIS smiles.

RABELAIS
We're meeting with Trimmer in an hour.

INT. A VERY SMALL OFFICE BUILDING-DAY

The THIRD DWARF slams his fist down on a table.

THIRD DWARF
(excited)
Fantastic!

THIRD DWARF
(continuing)
I'll meet you at the hotel.

The THIRD DWARF hangs up the phone.

EXT. BOARDWALK-ONE HOUR LATER

LIONEL is walking down the boardwalk toward the hotel.

TROY follows distantly behind him.

OTIS and RABELAIS greet him at the hotel entrance.

INT. SMALL HOTELROOM-DAY

OTIS and RABELAIS sit tapping their fingers on the couch.

They stare at LIONEL.

RABELAIS
(nervous)
So how are things?

LIONEL stares back them silently.

A small shadowy figure can be seen in the corner of the room.

THIRD DWARF
(impatient)
Enough!

The THIRD DWARF looks at LIONEL.

THIRD DWARF
(continuing)
I've waited a long time to meet you.

THIRD DWARF
(continuing)
Do you know why you're here?

EXT. DECK OUTSIDE THE SMALL HOTELROOM-DAY

TROY is standing on the deck listening.

An OLD WOMAN comes up behind him.

PALM READER
(to TROY)
Have you seen the future?

TROY stands there shocked, and shakes his head.

PALM READER
(continuing)
I didn't think so.

The PALM READER takes TROY'S hand, and then places her hand on his forehead.

EXT. STREET FAIR-NIGHT

MARIA is slumped over on the boardwalk. Sirens can be heard.

TROY pulls up in a police car.

He runs up to LIONEL, and places handcuffs on him. As he does LIONEL starts to disappear, and so does everything else.

The PALM READER removes her hand from TROY'S head, and he opens his eyes.

PALM READER
It could happen just that way.

The PALM READER snaps her fingers, and TROY disappears in a cloud of smoke.

The PALM READER bangs on the window.

INT. SMALL HOTELROOM-DAY

RABELAIS gets up to answer the knock. He walks over to the window, and pushes it open.

INT. DECK OUTSIDE THE SMALL HOTELROOM-DAY

RABELAIS is about to hand the PALM READER some money.

RABELAIS
(smiles)
Thanks--

RABELAIS pulls the money back, and then pulls a tiny pistol out of his coat.

RABELAIS
(continuing)
But your services are longer required.

RABELAIS fires his pistol.

The PALM READER slumps over.

RABELAIS snaps his fingers, and the PALM READER disappears in a cloud of smoke.

INT. SMALL HOTELROOM-DAY

THIRD DWARF
(to RABELAIS)
Is everything taken care of?

RABELAIS winks at him. The THIRD DWARF continues his conversation with LIONEL.

THIRD DWARF
(continuing)
Things have seemed a little strange lately?

LIONEL nods.

THIRD DWARF
(continuing)
You've heard of the Maria Caswell stories?

LIONEL nods again.

LIONEL
She's my girlfriend.

THIRD DWARF
(smiles)
That's right. Can I ask you another question Lionel?

LIONEL nods in agreement.

THIRD DWARF
(continuing)
Great. Now, you're a gambling man, aren't you Lionel?

LIONEL
Sure.

The THIRD DWARF takes a piece of paper from his pocket, and sets it on the table.

THIRD DWARF
Fine. I want to make a friendly wager with you Lionel. We play one hand of cards. If I win you grant me one favor.

LIONEL stops him.

LIONEL
What do I get if I win?

The THIRD DWARF snickers.

THIRD DWARF
Well, if you win, I'll give you the answers to make sense of the strangeness.

LIONEL
Who are you?

THIRD DWARF
That's all part of the answer. Do we have a bet?

The LANDLORD'S words again echo in LIONEL'S head.

We now see this figure more clearly, as the image of LIONEL'S father BUZZ.

LANDLORD/BUZZ
(grim smile)
Next time, don't bet more than you can afford to lose.

LIONEL feels the top of his head for his missing hat.

THIRD DWARF
Do we have a bet Mr. Trimmer?

LIONEL sits there in a trance, and shakes it off.

LIONEL
(weak smile)
Sure.

LIONEL and the THIRD DWARF shake hands.

THIRD DWARF
Sign this.

The THIRD DWARF puts the piece of paper in front of LIONEL.

LIONEL
What's this?

The THIRD DWARF smiles.

THIRD DWARF
An agreement between two gentlemen.

The THIRD DWARF hands LIONEL a pen.

LIONEL signs the paper, and removes a deck of cards from his pocket.

THIRD DWARF
(continuing)
Do you mind if I deal?

LIONEL places the deck in front of the THIRD DWARF.

LIONEL
Be my guest.

The THIRD DWARF starts shuffling, and drops the cards on the floor.

He and LIONEL both pick them up.

The THIRD DWARF places one card up his sleeve. LIONEL doesn't notice.

With lightning speed the THIRD DWARF deals out the cards face down.

THIRD DWARF
(smiles)
The suspense is killing me.

The THIRD DWARF turns over his card, to reveal an ACE.

LIONEL turns over his card, to reveal a KING.

A sad expression comes across LIONEL'S face.

LIONEL
What do I owe you?

The THIRD DWARF places a hand on LIONEL'S shoulder.

THIRD DWARF
First things first. I owe you some answers.

LIONEL
(baffled)
But I--

The THIRD DWARF smiles.

THIRD DWARF
I know you didn't win, but I'm required to give you the answers.

LIONEL shakes his head.

LIONEL
(puzzled)
Then why the card game?

THIRD DWARF
You owe me a favor now.

LIONEL nods.

THIRD DWARF
(continuing)
First, what is your take on things?

LIONEL
What?

THIRD DWARF
What do you think has been happening?

LIONEL shakes his head.

LIONEL
I dunno.

THIRD DWARF
It all started back when Harry Krumpnik was on the force.

LIONEL
The founder of the Wild West Casino?

The THIRD DWARF nods.

LIONEL
(continuing)
Force?

THIRD DWARF
You see Lionel, myself and others like me--

The THIRD DWARF points to OTIS and RABELAIS.

THIRD DWARF
(continuing)
We're part of a dream police force, known as the "keepers of the dream code."

LIONEL pinches himself.

LIONEL
You seem real enough.

The THIRD DWARF laughs.

THIRD DWARF
Dreams can't tell from dreams.

A confused look comes across LIONEL'S face.

LIONEL
What do you mean?

THIRD DWARF
(smiles)
I'm getting to that. You see Lionel, dreams will play out as they must. It's our job to see that they do.

LIONEL sits listening intently.

THIRD DWARF
(continuing)
Maria has been dreaming.

LIONEL
That explains why there are two of her.

THIRD DWARF
Exactly.

LIONEL
I got that far in the stories. What is she dreaming of?

THIRD DWARF
You.

LIONEL blushes.

LIONEL
It's nice to know I'm in her dreams.

THIRD DWARF
You don't understand. You are her dreams.

LIONEL gets up from the couch, and grabs the THIRD DWARF by the collar.

THIRD DWARF
(continuing)
Some people dream of peace, some chaos, and some want a little excitement. Who's more exciting than a cowboy? I think you know how this all turns out though.

LIONEL closes his eyes.

INT. A SMOKY KITCHEN-NIGHT

A group of MIDDLE AGED MEN are playing cards.

A LITTLE BOY watches them.

BUZZ
(screams)
Lionel! Daddy's working here!

The LITTLE BOY scampers off.

He stops at the television, and stares at the image of a western cowboy.

INT. POLICE ACADEMY BUILDING-DAY

TWO YOUNG MEN sit in cadets uniforms. One holds a newspaper tightly.

YOUNG LIONEL
(in tears)
Troy--I just can't believe it.
John Wayne--dead.

YOUNG LIONEL sits there twirling his gun.

YOUNG TROY
(sympathetic)
You're the last cowboy my friend.

EXT. A DARK ALLEY-EARLY MORNING

TWO YOUNG POLICE OFFICERS run down an alley.

One of them, YOUNG LIONEL, fires his pistol.

We see the image of a DEAD YOUNG BOY.

YOUNG LIONEL stands there in tears.

YOUNG LIONEL
(upset)
Ah, shit! Shit Troy!

YOUNG TROY places his hands on YOUNG LIONEL'S shoulders.

LIONEL
Ah. Man I'm a killer--a baby
killer.

Tears stream down LIONEL'S face.

YOUNG TROY
You're a cowboy.

EXT. BOARDWALK-EARLY MORNING

We see a YOUNG LIONEL get off a bus.

He walks past the WILD WEST CASINO, there is a HELP WANTED sign.

He goes inside.

YOUNG LIONEL is handed a cowboy outfit by a YOUNG WOMAN, MARIA.

EXT. BEACH-DAY

A YOUNGER LIONEL and MARIA frolic on the beach.

They embrace, and look into each other's eyes.

LIONEL
(mouths the words)
I love you.

EXT. SUBURBAN LAWN-DAY

A LITTLE GIRL sits at a picnic table. She is blowing out candles on a plain looking birthday cake.

She begins to open a present, and then we see that there are a stack of yellowed detective stories inside. She frowns.

INT. AN OFFICE BUILDING-DAY

We see a YOUNG MARIA filing some papers.

EXT. BOARDWALK-EARLY MORNING

We see a YOUNG MARIA get off a bus, and enter the WILD WEST CASINO.

EXT. BEACH-DAY

A YOUNGER LIONEL and MARIA frolic on the beach.

They embrace and look into each other's eyes.

MARIA
(mouths the words)
I love you.

EXT. WILD WEST CASINO-NIGHT

LIONEL and MARIA are talking to the CASINO MANAGER.

CASINO MANAGER
(beaming)
How would you guys like to work the street fair tonight?

LIONEL and MARIA stand there in silence.

CASINO MANAGER
(continuing)
Great!

EXT. STREET FAIR-NIGHT

LIONEL is sitting on a horse.

MARIA walks past him, and places an apple on her head.

LIONEL twirls his pistols.

The crowd cheers.

LIONEL'S fires his pistol.

The bullet splits the apple in half, the crowd cheers a second, and then everyone and everything starts to disappear except MARIA.

INT. SMALL HOTELROOM-DAY

LIONEL
Yeah. We know how this turns out.

THIRD DWARF
I thought so. Good. Now let me finish explaining things.

LIONEL
Sure.

THIRD DWARF
There are of course--alternate endings to any future.

LIONEL
(curious)
What do you mean alternate endings?

THIRD DWARF
Right now Lionel--all of this is theory. None of it's real. You and I--this whole world, it's a dream scape. That doesn't mean things can't change.

LIONEL
How do you mean change?

THIRD DWARF
I mean, this isn't reality for anyone.

LIONEL
What is?

The THIRD DWARF takes LIONEL'S hand, and places a hand on his head.

LIONEL
(continuing)
Not again.

The THIRD DWARF frowns.

THIRD DWARF
Close your eyes.

LIONEL closes his eyes.

EXT. STREET FAIR-NIGHT

LIONEL sits on a horse.

He is twirling a pair of pistols.

MARIA walks past him, and places an apple on her head.

LIONEL is about to fire his pistol, when his horse makes a jerking movement.

The gun goes off.

The bullet hits MARIA'S forehead.

MARIA slumps to the ground.

LIONEL runs over to her.

INT. SMALL HOTELROOM-DAY

The THIRD DWARF removes his hand from LIONEL'S head.

LIONEL opens his eyes.

THIRD DWARF
(to LIONEL)
Do you see what I mean about alternate endings?

LIONEL frowns.

THIRD DWARF
(continuing)
See Lionel, there are a few ways this whole thing could go. I would much prefer this second ending.

There is silence for a few seconds.

LIONEL
(stammers)
I, I--it's just--

The THIRD DWARF rolls his eyes.

THIRD DWARF
(sarcastic)
You think you love her? That's it, isn't it?

LIONEL is shaking.

LIONEL
(screams)
That's how I feel!

The THIRD DWARF slams his fist on the table in anger.

THIRD DWARF
(pissed)
It's not real! Any of it! You're not real! Don't be a damn fool!

LIONEL picks the THIRD DWARF up, and yells into his ear.

LIONEL
I won't do it!

The THIRD DWARF yells back.

THIRD DWARF
(laughing)
You have no choice!

LIONEL laughs this time.

LIONEL
There's always a choice! An alternate ending as you put.

The THIRD DWARF points to the piece of paper on the table.

THIRD DWARF
(smiles)
You owe me!

LIONEL drops the THIRD DWARF on the floor, and stands frozen.

THIRD DWARF
(continuing)
I'm calling in my favor.

LIONEL is now in tears.

LIONEL
(to the THIRD DWARF)
Not this.

OTIS and RABELAIS stand laughing at LIONEL.

THIRD DWARF
A favor--is a favor.

LIONEL continues to stand there sobbing.

The THIRD DWARF looks him in the eyes.

THIRD DWARF
(continuing)
Next time, don't bet more than you can afford to lose.

LIONEL stops crying and looks at him.

The THIRD DWARF snaps his fingers, and LIONEL disappears in a cloud of smoke.

INT. LIONEL'S APARTMENT-MORNING

An alarm clock is blaring.

LIONEL rolls out of bed, and falls on the floor.

He stumbles to the kitchen.

There is a loud banging noise.

LIONEL walks into the next room.

The front door bursts open.

It is about to smack him in the face, when he steps away.

His LANDLORD enters.

LANDLORD
Where's my money?!

Playing cards are scattered everywhere.

LIONEL reaches into his pocket, and produces some money.

The LANDLORD gives him a strange look.

LIONEL
(puzzled)
Is there a problem?

The LANDLORD looks at the money in LIONEL'S hand.

LANDLORD
(scowls)
I don't want your play money!

LIONEL looks at the money, and notices that it is very much play money.

LIONEL
Look, I'm--

The LANDLORD punches LIONEL in the stomach.

He doubles over in pain.

The LANDLORD removes a large pair of fuzzy dice from his coat, and proceeds to box LIONEL'S ears with them.

He takes LIONEL'S cowboy hat, and places it on his head.

LANDLORD
Next time, don't bet more than you can afford to lose.

LIONEL
(under his breath)
Where have I heard that before.

The LANDLORD exits.

LIONEL walks into the bedroom.

He glances at a framed photo of a YOUNG WOMAN, his girlfriend MARIA.

LIONEL removes some money from a purse sitting on the dresser.

He stands frozen for a few seconds.

LIONEL thinks twice about taking the money, and places it back in the purse.

MARIA is sleeping in bed.

LIONEL places a kiss on her cheek, and exits the room.

EXT. BOARDWALK-MORNING

LIONEL walks along the boardwalk.

He begins coughing, and looks at his watch. The face appears cracked, and it has stopped moving.

INT. THE IRISH PUB-MORNING

LIONEL walks inside. He is still coughing.

His friend TROY DEVENS sits at the bar. He motions LIONEL over.

LIONEL sets some money down on the bar.

TROY
(puzzled)
What's that for?

LIONEL
You were going to ask me for money.

TROY smirks.

TROY
No. I wasn't. I was going to ask you what happened yesterday.

LIONEL
(shocked)
You remember that?!

TROY laughs.

TROY
Who could forget it?

LIONEL is speechless.

TROY
(continuing)
So what happened in your meeting with the dwarf kingpin?

LIONEL
They're cops.

TROY
(smiles)
What?! We never saw anything like them at the academy.

LIONEL laughs.

LIONEL
Not that I recall.

TROY
Keep talking.

LIONEL
They refer to themselves as the "keepers of the dream code." Whatever that means.

TROY
(curious)
And?

LIONEL puts an arm around TROY'S shoulder.

LIONEL
Do you remember anything before the academy?

TROY sits scratching his head.

TROY
(stressed)
Everything has been a little cloudy lately.

LIONEL
(serious)
None of it's real!

TROY looks at LIONEL confused.

TROY
What are you talking about?!

LIONEL
That's what they told me! None of it's real! You and me!

LIONEL stops and takes a breath.

LIONEL
(continuing)
We just exist in some dream Maria's been having to make her life more exciting!

TROY pinches himself, and then LIONEL.

TROY
(smiles)
I just wanted to see if either of us were dreaming.

LIONEL
We're the dream!

TROY sets his head down on the bar.

TROY
(sad)
Shit.

TROY
(continuing)
You mean I don't have a family?

LIONEL pats TROY on the back.

LIONEL
You aren't you--I'm not me either.

TROY lifts his head.

TROY
You aren't a cowboy?

LIONEL laughs.

LIONEL
I'm still a cowboy--I just don't exist.

TROY
(sarcastic)
Great.

LIONEL
We have to find Maria.

LIONEL rushes out of the PUB.

TROY follows behind him.

EXT. BOARDWALK-MORNING

LIONEL runs down the boardwalk with TROY in tow.

TROY
(panting)
What's the hurry? Why do you have to find Maria this second?

LIONEL
I'm supposed to kill her.

TROY jumps on top of LIONEL, knocking him over.

TROY
(shocked)
What did you just say?

LIONEL looks at TROY with a stern expression.

LIONEL
I didn't mention that?

TROY raises an eyebrow.

TROY
No--you didn't.

LIONEL
Listen, if I kill her in the dream, she's dead for real.

LIONEL
(continuing)
You and I become the reality.

A crazed expression comes across LIONEL'S face.

TROY
I can't let you do that.

LIONEL stares at TROY.

LIONEL
What?! Why not?

A look of fright comes across TROY'S face.

TROY
You really want to kill Maria?!

LIONEL thinks of MARIA snoring in bed.

LIONEL
There are two of them!

TROY becomes confused.

TROY
Two of what?

LIONEL
Maria! There are two Marias!

TROY
(screaming)
And you're going to kill them both! You said so yourself!

LIONEL starts sobbing.

LIONEL
I don't have a choice!

TROY looks LIONEL in the eyes.

TROY
There's always another way!

LIONEL pushes TROY away from him.

LIONEL
There are no alternate endings here Troy! I did something stupid!

TROY
Whatever it is--we can fix it!

LIONEL
I made a bet with the dwarf kingpin!

TROY becomes very calm.

TROY
What?

LIONEL stops sobbing.

LIONEL
We had a wager.

TROY
What do you mean wager?

LIONEL shrugs.

LIONEL
The main dwarf and I played a game of cards.

LIONEL
(continuing)
If I won, they'd explain why things had been so strange lately.

LIONEL stops to clear his throat.

TROY
And if he won?

LIONEL
(sighs)
I'd kill Maria. Which apparently is part of the dream, at least one version of it.

TROY
I thought you said there were no alternate endings?

TROY stands there waving his arms around.

TROY
(continuing)
This is just great! You do know that I can't let you do this, right?

LIONEL nods.

LIONEL
(sobs)
I really don't have any choice here Troy. I lost the game.

TROY stands there thinking for a few seconds.

TROY
What's that phrase that you told me your father used to say?

TROY stands there thinking about it, and then snaps his fingers.

TROY
(continuing)
I got it!

LIONEL lowers his head in shame.

LIONEL
Next time, don't bet more than you can afford to lose.

TROY smiles.

TROY
That's it!

LIONEL shoots an angry look at TROY.

LIONEL
Don't you get it?!

TROY
What?!

LIONEL
There isn't going to be any next

time! Not if I don't kill Maria!

LIONEL stands there pulling at his hair.

LIONEL
(continuing)
Either way--I'm dead. If I kill Maria, I kill my heart. If Maria lives, I cease to exist.

TROY removes some handcuffs from his pocket, and puts them around LIONEL'S wrist.

TROY
(smiles)
I'm still a cop--there are certain things I can't let you do.

INT. LOCAL JAIL-DAY

LIONEL is sitting in jail.

TROY is sitting on a wooden chair outside his cell.

A GUARD sits at a desk beside him.

TROY
(to the GUARD)
You can go home Rick. I've got a handle on things here.

The GUARD exits.

TROY
(continuing)
So.

LIONEL
So.

TROY
This is what the last night of existence feels like.

LIONEL
Yeah. Do you think we might be able to listen to the radio?

We see a radio on the GUARD'S desk.

TROY
Sure.

TROY turns on the radio.

LIONEL
A little higher?

TROY turns the radio up a few notches.

EXT. OUTSIDE THE JAIL-DAY

OTIS and RABELAIS sit outside the JAIL with tiny hammers.

They bang at the wall.

INT. LOCAL JAIL-DAY

LIONEL and TROY sit listening to the radio. The music is very loud.

EXT. OUTSIDE THE JAIL-DAY

OTIS and RABELAIS continue to hammer at the wall.

OTIS stops.

OTIS
(to RABELAIS)
I can hear music coming from somewhere.

RABELAIS just shrugs.

RABELAIS
I work better to music.

INT. LOCAL JAIL-DAY

LIONEL notices a small crack in the wall.

The head of a tiny hammer comes through.

EXT. OUTSIDE THE JAIL-DAY

OTIS
(excited)
You did it!

OTIS hugs RABELAIS. Then they proceed to make the crack larger, and then go into the cell.

INT. LOCAL JAIL-DAY

TROY stops listening to the music, and notices OTIS and RABELAIS in the cell.

OTIS
(to TROY)
Hey, there.

TROY is about to pull out his gun, when RABELAIS pulls a tiny pistol on him.

RABELAIS
(laughs)
Easy there big fella.

TROY stops in his tracks.

OTIS
(to LIONEL)
The boss had us tail you.

LIONEL shakes OTIS'S hand.

LIONEL
Let's get out of here.

LIONEL and OTIS exit the JAIL.

RABELAIS keeps the gun on TROY.

EXT. WILD WEST CASINO-DAY

LIONEL is running toward the WILD WEST CASINO.

He sees MARIA standing outside.

He plants a passionate kiss on her lips.

She gives him a strange look, and slaps him.

LIONEL
(confused)
What the--

MARIA
Who are you?

LIONEL starts throwing his hands up in the air.

MARIA stops him, and places her hand on his shoulders.

MARIA
(continuing)
Calm down! Do you have a match?

LIONEL rolls his eyes.

LIONEL
(tried)
Christ--not this again.

MARIA
(confused)
What?!

He looks at her cigarette.

LIONEL
You don't smoke.

MARIA
All I wanted was a match.

LIONEL
We have some in the apartment.

MARIA throws her hands up in the air.

MARIA
(pissed)
What are you talking about?!

LIONEL starts pacing around in a panic.

LIONEL
(yells)
This isn't funny anymore!

INT. WILD WEST CASINO-SAME MOMENT

OTIS and RABELAIS are sitting at slot machines by a window. They watch as LIONEL continues to pace back and forth.

EXT. OUTSIDE THE CASINO-DAY

MARIA places her hands on LIONEL'S shoulders to stop his pacing.

MARIA
It's my first day here! I'm nervous enough!

LIONEL stops in his tracks.

LIONEL
(flustered)
I've got a bottle of scotch.

MARIA softens.

MARIA
(slight smile)
Is that an invitation?

LIONEL starts walking in silence toward his apartment.

MARIA
(continuing)
Do you always go around kissing total strangers?

OTIS and RABELAIS trail behind them.

INT. CLUB WET DREAMS-DAY

LIONEL and MARIA walk through the strip club below LIONEL'S apartment.

LIONEL
Would you like a drink?

MARIA
Shouldn't we be getting back to work?

LIONEL sits down at a table.

A waitress comes, and sets two napkins down on the table.

LIONEL
(serious)
You really don't remember me?

MARIA shakes her head, and gets up to leave.

MARIA
(pissed)
Not this again!

LIONEL
(shocked)
You always remember!

LIONEL points upward.

LIONEL
(continuing)
Our place is upstairs.

MARIA starts walking away. LIONEL decides to play along again.

LIONEL
(continuing)
Fine. We've never met. I just wish we had.

MARIA begins to talk.

MARIA
I'm from--

LIONEL
(smiles)
Sioux City, Iowa.

MARIA is now slightly frightened.

MARIA
How did you--

LIONEL
I'll explain everything upstairs.

LIONEL gets up to leave. MARIA follows him.

MARIA
Can I use your bathroom?

INT. LIONEL'S APARTMENT-DAY

LIONEL and MARIA enter the apartment.

LIONEL shows MARIA where the bathroom is.

LIONEL enters his bedroom to get his spare cowboy hat.

MARIA continues to talk to him from the bathroom.

MARIA
So how long have you been working at the casino?

MARIA comes out of the bathroom, and enters the bedroom.

Snoring can be heard.

We see the other MARIA sleeping in LIONEL'S bed.

MARIA walks over to the bed.

MARIA
(continuing)
That's--

LIONEL
You.

MARIA
Yeah!

MARIA faints.

She falls on the floor before LIONEL can catch her.

LIONEL
Ah, shit.

INT. LIONEL'S APARTMENT-A LITTLE LATER

A tea kettle blares.

MARIA'S eyes open.

She sits rubbing her head.

LIONEL stands above her.

MARIA
(upset)
What's going on?! Who are you?!

LIONEL
I could ask you the same thing.

MARIA
How do you know me?!

LIONEL
We met about a year ago. We've lived here about 3 months.

MARIA paces around the room.

LIONEL grabs a hold of her. He slaps her.

LIONEL
(continuing)
You're making me nervous.

LIONEL sits down on the floor.

MARIA sits next to him.

LIONEL
(continuing)
You really don't remember?

MARIA nods.

LIONEL
(continuing)
The name's Lionel, Lionel Trimmer.

MARIA points to the spitting image of herself snoring in the bed.

MARIA
Well, Who's that?

LIONEL sighs.

LIONEL
That's a reasonable question.

INT. LIONEL'S APARTMENT-A LITTLE LATER

LIONEL has just finished telling MARIA what's going on.

MARIA
(serious)
So. What do you plan to do?

LIONEL
(smiles)
I can't kill you.

MARIA hugs him, and points to the sleeping MARIA.

MARIA
(smiles)
That's from both of us.

LIONEL
Thanks.

MARIA
You're serious now--you aren't going to try to kill me when I turn my back?

LIONEL laughs.

LIONEL
You're just going to have to trust me.

MARIA touches LIONEL'S face.

MARIA
You don't look like a killer.

INT. CLUB WET DREAMS-DAY

OTIS and RABELAIS are sitting in the strip club again.

OTIS
(to RABELAIS)
Did I mention that this was supposed to be my vacation week?

RABELAIS lets out a long sigh.

INT. LIONEL'S APARTMENT-DAY

LIONEL and MARIA are still talking.

LIONEL
Now all we have to do is make it to the street fair.

INT. CLUB WET DREAMS-DAY

OTIS sits staring at a stripper.

RABELAIS
Did you put a wire on him?

OTIS
(distracted)
What?

RABELAIS
Did you put a wire on him?

OTIS laughs.

OTIS
Of course.

RABELAIS
What are they talking about?

OTIS
He just said that he wasn't going to kill her.

OTIS and RABELAIS look at each other at the same time.

OTIS & RABELAIS
(together)
Shit!

OTIS laughs nervously.

OTIS
Maybe he's fooling her?

RABELAIS gives OTIS a confused look.

RABELAIS
What do you mean?

OTIS
Maybe he's just trying to get her on his side. You know, to make things easier.

RABELAIS let's out a long breath.

RABELAIS
(sarcastic)
Yeah. And maybe you're tall too.

OTIS gives RABELAIS a dirty look.

LIONEL and MARIA come walking down the stairs into the club.

MARIA walks outside.

LIONEL looks back at OTIS and RABELAIS. He gives them a thumbs up.

They raise two foam fingers that spell out "kill her."

LIONEL walks outside.

OTIS
(to RABELAIS)
What do you think?

RABELAIS
(frowns)
I don't trust him.

OTIS nods in agreement.

They exit the club.

INT. WILD WEST CASINO-NIGHT

LIONEL and MARIA stand talking to the CASINO MANAGER.

CASINO MANAGER
(beaming)
How would you guys like to work the street fair tonight?

LIONEL and MARIA stand there in silence.

CASINO MANAGER
(continuing)
Great!

EXT. OUTSIDE THE CASINO-NIGHT

LIONEL and MARIA stand outside of the CASINO.

MARIA
(to LIONEL)
What now?

LIONEL stands there thinking.

MARIA hands him a brush for his horse.

LIONEL
I'll be right back. I have to go to the bathroom.

INT. WILD WEST CASINO-NIGHT

LIONEL is heading toward the bathroom, when he notices a card game. He decides to sit.

OTIS and RABELAIS come up behind him.

LIONEL
(startled)
Hey, fellas.

OTIS
(pissed)
Get on with the killing!

LIONEL appears very distracted.

LIONEL
I will--after this hand.

OTIS and RABELAIS attempt to pull him away from the table.

TROY comes up behind them.

TROY
(serious)
Nobody's goin' to kill anyone.

RABELAIS looks at TROY.

RABELAIS
(sighs)
Not you again.

OTIS
(to RABELAIS)
You should have shot him!

RABELAIS nods.

TROY pulls a gun on everyone.

RABELAIS
(scoffs)
You can't kill us all!

TROY points to LIONEL.

TROY
(laughs)
If he dies--you cease to exist right now.

OTIS and RABELAIS shut up.

TROY grabs LIONEL'S arm.

TROY
(continuing)
Come with me.

TROY looks at OTIS and RABELAIS as well.

TROY
(continuing)
All of you.

OTIS, RABELAIS, LIONEL, and TROY exit the casino.

EXT. OUTSIDE THE CASINO-NIGHT

MARIA stands outside waiting for LIONEL.

MARIA
(to LIONEL)
What's going on?

TROY looks to MARIA.

TROY
Don't you worry about these three.

LIONEL whispers to TROY.

LIONEL
We have to talk.

TROY looks LIONEL over.

TROY
(sighs)
You have one minute.

LIONEL starts whispering into TROY'S ear.

LIONEL
I'm not going to kill her.

TROY shrugs.

TROY
How do I know that you’re telling me the truth?

LIONEL shrugs this time.

LIONEL
You don't. I guess you're just going to have to trust me.

TROY looks into LIONEL'S eyes.

TROY
You don't have the face of a killer.

LIONEL hugs TROY.

LIONEL
More like a cowboy?

TROY
More like a cowboy.

LIONEL runs over to MARIA.

MARIA
(to LIONEL)
Let's get ourselves to that street fair.

LIONEL and MARIA leave.

TROY turns his attention to OTIS and RABELAIS.

TROY
(smiles)
What do I do with the two of you?

OTIS and RABELAIS shake their heads in uncertainty.

EXT. STREET FAIR-NIGHT

LIONEL and MARIA are standing waiting for the crowd to fill in.

INT. TROY'S APARTMENT-NIGHT

TROY is sitting with OTIS and RABELAIS watching "The MALTESE FALCON" on television.

OTIS
(pissed)
This movie sucks!

OTIS throws a piece of popcorn at the screen.

TROY punches OTIS'S shoulder.

TROY
(nudges OTIS)
Let me tell you something, you could learn a few things from old Sam Spade.

RABELAIS laughs.

TROY
(continuing)
What are you laughing at?

TROY points to OTIS.

TROY
(continuing)
You're worse than he is.

We see that OTIS and RABELAIS are handcuffed to TROY'S couch.

TROY
(continuing)
I'm going to get the other bag of popcorn. You guys behave.

TROY exits the room.

EXT. STREET FAIR-NIGHT

LIONEL is twirling a pistol.

MARIA walks past him, and places an apple on her head.

INT. TROY'S APARTMENT-NIGHT

TROY walks back into the room. The arm is ripped off of his couch, and OTIS and RABELAIS are nowhere to be found.

TROY feels a draft. He looks at his front window. It is wide open.

TROY
Shit.

TROY starts attempting to rip his hair out.

EXT. BOARDWALK-NIGHT

We see OTIS and RABELAIS wandering down the boardwalk.

A YOUNG BOY is on a scooter. RABELAIS points a gun at him, and he drops the scooter.

OTIS and RABELAIS get on the scooter, and ride down the boardwalk in search of the STREET FAIR.

EXT. BOARDWALK-A WHILE LATER

OTIS and RABELAIS are still wandering down the boardwalk.

OTIS
(sad expression)
We're lost.

RABELAIS
(sarcastic)
No shit.

They stop pushing the scooter.

OTIS
Are you going to ask for directions?

RABELAIS face turns red.

RABELAIS
(pissed)
Why me?

OTIS
(shrugs)
It's your thing.

RABELAIS
You're the one that got us lost!

OTIS just stands there in silence.

RABELAIS starts choking him.

RABELAIS
(continuing)
If we still exist tomorrow--I'm really going to kill you.

EXT. STREET FAIR-NIGHT

LIONEL and MARIA are about to start their act, when TROY approaches. He has a troubled expression on his face.

LIONEL
(concerned)
What's wrong?

LIONEL steadies his horse.

MARIA removes the apple from her head.

TROY
(to LIONEL)
They got away.

LIONEL
(confused)
Got away?

TROY
(lowers his head)
The dwarfs.

MARIA walks over to them.

MARIA
How did they manage that?

TROY keeps his head lowered.

TROY
I went for popcorn.

LIONEL and MARIA look at each other. Then they turn their attentions over to TROY again.

MARIA
(to TROY)
What now?

TROY shakes his head.

TROY
I dunno.

MARIA starts pacing back and forth.

MARIA
(to LIONEL)
Should we continue the act?

LIONEL remains silent for a few seconds.

MARIA
(continuing)
Well?!

LIONEL
(smiles)
Let's do it. They may not even be able to find us.

LIONEL kisses MARIA.

He gets up on the horse.

MARIA again walks past him, and places the apple on her head. LIONEL twirls his pistols.

The crowd cheers.

LIONEL prepares to fire his gun.

EXT. BOARDWALK-SAME MOMENT

OTIS and RABELAIS are looking around when they hear music, and some cheering.

They turn a corner.

EXT. STREET FAIR-NIGHT

OTIS and RABELAIS approach the crowd.

RABELAIS incites them to do "the wave".

OTIS yells out.

OTIS
(yells)
Kill her!

The crowd laughs at OTIS. They start chanting.

CROWD
(chanting)
Kill her!

LIONEL stops. He gives OTIS and the CROWD a dirty look.

CROWD
(continuing)
Kill her!

LIONEL raises his pistol.

He aims at the apple.

Before he can fire OTIS removes a tiny gun from his pocket.

LIONEL looks back.

LIONEL
(screams)
No!

LIONEL fires a shot at OTIS.

It hits him just before his own bullet hits MARIA in the side of the face.

LIONEL runs over to her.

MARIA looks into LIONEL'S eyes.

MARIA
(serious)
You have to get back up on that horse. We have to finish the act in order for things to go full circle.

LIONEL takes MARIA'S hand.

LIONEL
You're in no--

MARIA squeezes LIONEL'S hand.

MARIA
(forceful)
Get back on the horse. There are no alternate endings.

LIONEL helps MARIA up. She places the apple on her head.

LIONEL gets back up on his horse.

RABELAIS stands over a weakened OTIS.

RABELAIS
(frantic)
Would someone please call an ambulance?!

LIONEL again raises his pistol.

The CROWD still chants.

CROWD
(chanting)
Kill her! Kill her!

TROY fires his gun to calm them down.

They stop chanting.

LIONEL fires his pistol.

The apple is split in half.

The CROWD cheers.

LIONEL waves his hat in the air.

He rides his horse over to MARIA.

LIONEL'S image begins to fade.

He gets off of the horse, and places a kiss on MARIA'S hand as he disappears.

A few seconds later TROY, OTIS, RABELAIS, and the CROWD disappear as well.

MARIA stands alone.

INT. MARIA'S APARTMENT-MORNING

An alarm clock blares.

MARIA rolls out of bed, and stumbles to the kitchen. She is wearing a wrinkled business suit.

She walks into the living room.

A cowboy western is playing on her television.

She smiles, turns off the television, and walks into the next room.

FADE OUT:

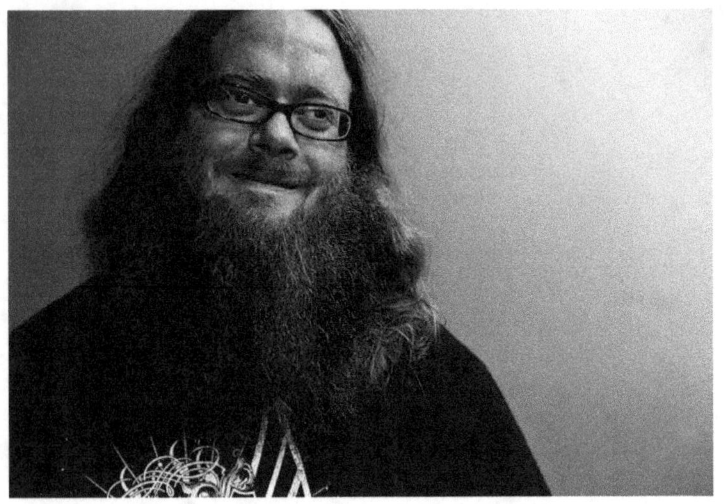

John Dorsey is the writer of more than 25 screenplays. He is a graduate of the now defunct, but still legendary, Writing for Film & Television program which operated at the University of the Arts in Philadelphia from 1996-2016. He is the writer of the recently produced feature film ***Missouri Loves Company*** and an Associate Producer on the upcoming film ***Tales from the Dead Zone***, starring Corey Feldman. He may be reached at archerevans@yahoo.com.

www.ingramcontent.com/pod-product-compliance
Lightning Source LLC
LaVergne TN
LVHW061250100826
845148LV00008B/1080
* 9 7 8 1 7 3 6 9 5 9 6 2 6 *